MAGIC DOOR TO LEARNING

Max's Math Machine

Written by Larry Dane Brimner • Illustrated by Robert Squier

Published in the United States of America by The Child's World®
PO Box 326 • Chanhassen, MN 55317-0326
800-599-READ • www.childsworld.com

Reading Adviser

Cecilia Minden-Cupp, PhD, Director of Language and Literacy, Harvard University Graduate School of Education, Cambridge, Massachusetts

Acknowledgments

The Child's World®: Mary Berendes, Publishing Director

Editorial Directions, Inc.: E. Russell Primm, Editorial Director and Project Manager; Katie Marsico, Associate Editor; Judith Shiffer, Assistant Editor; Matt Messbarger, Editorial Assistant

The Design Lab: Kathleen Petelinsek, Design and Art Production

Library of Congress Cataloging-in-Publication Data

Brimner, Larry Dane.
Max's math machine / written by Larry Dane Brimner ; illustrated by Robert Squier.
p. cm. – (Magic door to learning)
Summary: Young Max has invented a machine for adding and counting everything from shoes and socks piled on the floor to a school lunch with too many peas. Told in simple rhyming text.
ISBN 1-59296-522-9 (library bound : alk. paper) [1. Counting–Fiction. 2. Addition–Fiction. 3. Stories in rhyme.] I. Squier, Robert, ill. II. Title.
PZ8.3.B77145Max 2005
[E]–dc22 2005005371

A book is a door, a magic door.
It can take you places
you have never been before.
Ready? Set?
Turn the page.
Open the door.
Now it is time to explore.

Max was an inventor.

Max was tinkering in his bedroom. He took some scraps. He took some bits. He put many things together with nuts and bolts and tape. Max had invented a math machine.

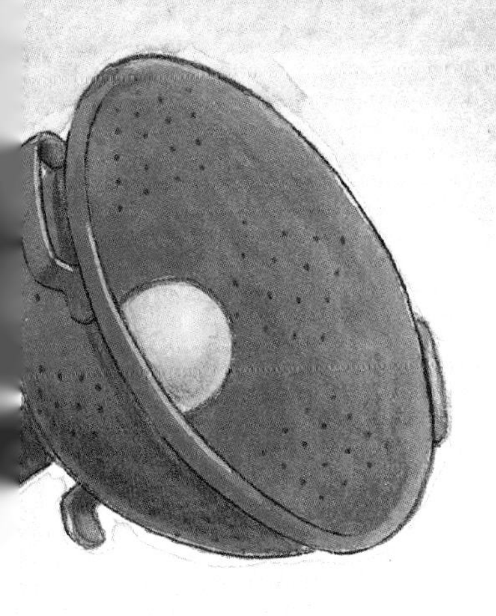

Max's math machine could count. Point it. Click it. Max's math machine would add things up.

Max pointed the machine at his shoes. *Click!* Is it true that one and one are two? Yes, that is true!

1+1=2

Max pointed his machine at a pile of socks. *Click!* One and two are three. Where do you think the fourth sock could be?

2+1=3

Max took his machine to school. It counted kids on swings and lots of other fun things.

2+2=4 · 3+2=5
4+1=5

Max's machine counted nests
in the trees and a hive with bees.

5+1=6 · 3+4=7
3+4=

He counted Anna's lunch
with too many peas.

4+4=8

Click! It counted buses
at the end of the day.

6+4=10

You can be like Max's machine if you try. How many hands on the bus are waving good-bye?

Our story is over, but there is still much to explore beyond the magic door!

Do you want to play a counting game? How many desks are in the classroom? How many chairs? You can even count the pieces of chalk! Have your friends do the same. Do your counts match?

These books will help you explore at the library and at home:

Elliott, David, and True Kelley (illustrator). *Hazel Nutt, Mad Scientist.* New York: Holiday House, 2003.

Milne, A.A. *Pooh Invents a New Game.* New York: Dutton Children's Books, 1991.

About the Author

Larry Dane Brimner is an award-winning author of more than 120 books for children. When he isn't at his computer writing, he can be found biking in Colorado or hiking in Arizona. You can visit him online at *www.brimner.com.*

About the Illustrator

Long before he could add, Robert Squier was drawing dinosaurs and superheroes. Today, after years of practice, he works as a graphic designer and illustrator. His illustrations appear in magazines, books, and on the occasional theater poster. He lives in Portsmouth, New Hampshire.